KU-100-496

Life Sentence

Brandon Robshaw

Published in association with
The Basic Skills Agency

Hodder & Stoughton
A MEMBER OF THE HODDER HEADLINE GROUP

Acknowledgements
Cover: Lee Stinton
Illustrations: Mike Bell

Orders: please contact Bookpoint Ltd, 39 Milton Park, Abingdon, Oxon OX14
4TD. Telephone: (44) 01235 400414, Fax: (44) 01235 400454. Lines are open
from 9.00–6.00, Monday to Saturday, with a 24 hour message answering service.
Email address: orders@bookpoint.co.uk

British Library Cataloguing in Publication Data
A catalogue record for this title is available from The British Library

ISBN 0 340 74237 2

First published 1999
Impression number   10 9 8 7 6 5 4 3 2 1
Year   2004 2003 2002 2001 2000 1999

Copyright © 1999 Brandon Robshaw

All rights reserved. No part of this publication may be reproduced or transmitted
in any form or by any means, electronic or mechanical, including photocopy,
recording, or any information storage and retrieval system, without permission in
writing from the publisher or under licence from the Copyright Licensing Agency
Limited. Further details of such licences (for reprographic reproduction) may be
obtained from the Copyright Licensing Agency Limited, of 90 Tottenham Court
Road, London W1P 9HE.

Typeset by Fakenham Photosetting Ltd, Fakenham, Norfolk.
Printed in Great Britain for Hodder & Stoughton Educational, a division of
Hodder Headline Plc, 338 Euston Road, London NW1 3BH by Athenaeum Press,
Gateshead, Tyne & Wear.

Life Sentence

Contents

1

Goodbye

'Goodbye, Mike.'
'Goodbye, Mum,' said Mike.

They were standing outside the school gates.
A sign said:
'Semper Boarding School.
Headmaster: Dr A. J. Dadd.'

Mike didn't like the look of the school.
The tall gates and iron railings
made it look like a prison.
The school building
was at the end of a long drive.
It was half hidden by dark, ugly trees.

Mike didn't want to go to boarding school.
But there was no choice.
His father was in the army
and had been posted abroad.
Mike's mother was flying out to join him.

She hugged Mike tightly.
'I hope you'll be happy here.'
'I'm sure I will,' said Mike.
He didn't want to alarm her
with his worries.

'I'll see you at Christmas,'
said his mother.
'OK, Mum. See you at Christmas.'

They kissed.
She got into her car and drove away.
Mike waved until she was out of sight.

Then he pushed open the gate.
It clanged shut behind him.
There was nobody about.
Everything was still and quiet.
The only sound was Mike's footsteps,
crunching on the gravel,
as he walked up the drive
towards the school.

2

The Prefect

Mike walked up the steps
and pushed open the door.
He found himself in
a large, empty hall.
There was still nobody about.

Then he heard footsteps,
echoing in the empty hall.
A tall figure in school uniform
came into sight.

He walked towards Mike.
He had a smooth, pale face
and short dark hair.
It was impossible to say
how old he was.

'Welcome to Semper,' he said.
'You must be Mike Potter.'

Mike nodded.

'I'm Terry Johnson. I'm a prefect here.
It's my job to show you around.'

'I'm glad to see you,' said Mike.
'I thought I'd come to a ghost school!'

'Oh, there are no ghosts here,' said Terry.
He laughed.

'But where is everyone?'

'They're all in class.
Where you'll be, soon.
I'll just show you round first.
Follow me.'

He placed his hand on Mike's shoulder
and led him across the hall.
They came to a heavy wooden door.
Terry turned the handle.
The door opened with a creak.

'After you,' said Terry.

3

The Latin Class

Mike went through into a long,
dimly-lit corridor.
Terry closed the heavy door
behind them.

Mike heard a strange sound.
It sounded like people chanting.
Mike couldn't understand what
they were chanting about.
It was in a language he didn't know.

'What's that noise?' he asked.

'They're learning their Latin,' said Terry.
'Want to have a look?'

They came to a door
with a glass pane in it.
Mike looked through.
Rows of pupils in uniform
were all chanting
Latin words together.

It was hard to be sure in the dim light,
but they all looked surprisingly old.
They must be Year 12 or 13,
thought Mike.
But some looked even older than that.
One looked as if he was going bald.
Was it a trick of the light?

'They're a bit old, aren't they?' asked Mike.
Terry didn't answer this.
He just laughed and walked on.

Mike caught him up.

He felt uneasy.

The classroom scene had disturbed him.

'What do you think of it here?'

he asked Terry.

'Do you like it?'

Terry laughed again.

'You get used to it.'

'Will I have to learn Latin?'

'Oh yes. Don't you know any?'

'Not a word.'

'So you don't know

what "Semper" means?'

asked Terry.

'No – what does it mean?'

'You'll find out,' said Terry.

'Come on, I'll show you the gym.'

4

The Gym

The gym looked as if
it hadn't been used for years.
Dust covered the wooden floor.
The paint was peeling off the walls.
Cobwebs hung from the ceiling.

Mike stared in amazement.
'Doesn't anyone ever use this?'

'Not really,' said Terry.
'They're too old, most of them.'

'What do you mean, too old?'

'I mean, not young,' explained Terry.
'Getting on a bit.
It's nice to get a young kid like you here.
It makes a change.'

'I'm not that young!' said Mike.
'I'm 14.'

'I remember being 14,' said Terry.
He laughed.
'Long time ago now.
Come on – I'll show you
the swimming pool.'

The swimming pool was in
a large room next door.
It wasn't much use
for swimming in, though.
There was no water in it.
Just a few patches of green slime
on the bottom.
The tiles were cracked,
with weeds poking through.

'Is this a joke?' asked Mike.
'How could anyone swim in this?
There's no water!'

'Oh, we don't swim in it,' said Terry.
'Not since the gym teacher
drowned himself in it.'

Mike began to feel scared.
Everything about this school was strange.

Terry was strange.

Perhaps he was mad.

Then Mike remembered –

it was the custom to play tricks

on new boys at school.

That's all it was.

Terry was winding him up.

Trying to scare him.

Well, it wouldn't work.

'Thanks for the tour,' Mike said.

'I've seen enough now.

I'd like to go and see the Head.'

'Good idea,' said Terry.

'I was just going to suggest it myself.

Let's go and see Dr Dadd.

You'll love Dr Dadd.

We all love Dr Dadd,' said Terry, laughing.

'He's like a father to us.'

5

Dr Dadd

They stood outside Dr Dadd's door.
It was a dark, heavy door
with 'Dr Dadd: Headmaster'
written on it in gold letters.
Terry knocked.
'Come in,' said a thin, high voice.

Dr Dadd was the oldest person
Mike had ever seen.
His head was completely bald.
His face was grey and wrinkled,
like a piece of old leather.
He had no teeth
and his cheeks were sunken in.
He peered at Mike
through the thick, dusty lenses
of his spectacles.

'Who's this?'

'It's the new boy, sir,' said Terry.
'His name's Mike Potter.'
'I see,' said Dr Dadd.
'Well, I hope you'll be
very happy here, Potter.'
Terry laughed.
'Shut up, Johnson!' said Dr Dadd.

'There's nothing funny about it.
He will be happy here.
Won't you, Potter?'

Mike said nothing.
He felt so lost and lonely
it brought a lump to his throat.
He hated Terry's constant laughter
and Dr Dadd's thin, high voice.
He felt as if he was trapped in a nightmare.

'Don't be shy, Potter!' said Dr Dadd.
'Speak up! Or I'll hit you
with my cane!'
He pulled open a drawer,
took out a cane
and laid it on the desk.
'I said, you'll be happy here –
won't you?'

It was too much for Mike.
He couldn't stand it any more.
He turned and ran from the room.

6

Escape?

He ran down the corridor
as fast as he could.
He came to a flight of stairs.
He ran up them.
He didn't know where he was going –
he just had to get away
from Terry and Dr Dadd.

He passed a window.
Through it, he saw the town –
shops, roads, churches, trees
and the river winding its way between
the buildings.
It all looked so free, so normal.
Mike longed to be out there,
away from this horrible school.

He ran on, searching for a way out.
He ran past a classroom.
The sight he saw was so strange, so mad,
that he had to stop and look.

It was a class of the oldest pupils
Mike had ever seen.
They looked even older than Dr Dadd.
There were men with long grey beards.
There were wrinkled, white-haired old women.
Some were so old
you couldn't tell if they were
men or women.

Some were reading, some were writing.
Some were talking to themselves.
Some were staring into space.

The teacher lay slumped over his desk.
A fly buzzed around his head.
Was he dead?

Slowly, the old people noticed
that Mike was there.
Their wrinkled old faces
turned to stare at him.

Mike turned and ran.
He had to get out of this place.
He came to another flight of stairs.
He ran down it.

At the bottom, he came to the corridor
that Terry had taken him through.
He heard the sound of chanting again.
Now he knew where he was.
He could escape.

7

The Gates

Mike ran through the corridor.
He ran through the hall
and out of the door.
He ran down the steps and down the drive
towards the gates.
The wind blew through his hair.
He was free – or almost.
He just had to get through the gates –
and then he'd never come back
to this place again.

He reached the gates.
'Semper Boarding School.
Headmaster: Dr A. J. Dadd,'
said the sign.
Mike pulled at the gates.
They didn't open.

He tugged at the gates
and shook them like a mad thing.
It was no use.
The gates were locked.
He looked up at the high railings.
There was no way he could climb them.
There was no way he could get out.

He heard a noise and looked round
in a panic.

Terry Johnson and Dr Dadd
were walking down the drive towards him.

8

What 'Semper' Meant

They took him by the arms.
Mike struggled,
but it was no use.
Dr Dadd might be old,
but there was a horrible strength
in his skinny arms.

'Let me go!' screamed Mike.

'Come along, Potter,' said Dr Dadd.
'It's time you were in class.'

They dragged him up the drive.

'I don't want to go to class!'
screamed Mike.
'This place is mad.
I saw a class full of old men and women.
What's going on here?'

'That was probably year 80,' said Terry.
'They're the oldest.'

'What? What do you mean?'

'Haven't you got it yet?' said Terry.
'When you come to this school,
you stay for ever.
That's why it's called "Semper".'

'What? What does that mean?'

'Don't you know any Latin, Potter?'
asked Dr Dadd in his thin, high voice.
'I can see we'll have to work on you.
"Semper" is Latin for "always".'

'You're here for always now,' said Terry.
'Well, until you die, anyway.'
He laughed.
'You'll get used to it.'

Mike started to scream again.
He was still screaming
as they dragged him up the steps.

The door slammed shut behind them.